BIRD BOY

AND OTHER SHORT STORIES

BIRD BOY

AND OTHER SHORT STORIES

Not every story needs a ghost or monster...
... to be scary

JORDAN MURRAY

This collection is a work of fiction. Any references to historical events, legitimate people, and legitimate places are used fictitiously. The remaining names, characters, and places are products of the author's imagination. Any resemblances to reality are purely coincidental.

First printed October 2020

This hardcover edition October 2021

Cover design by Jordan Murray via Book Cover Zone
Interior design and formatting by Jordan Murray

ISBN Hardcover: 978-1-7771060-2-7
ISBN Paperback: 978-1-7771060-1-0

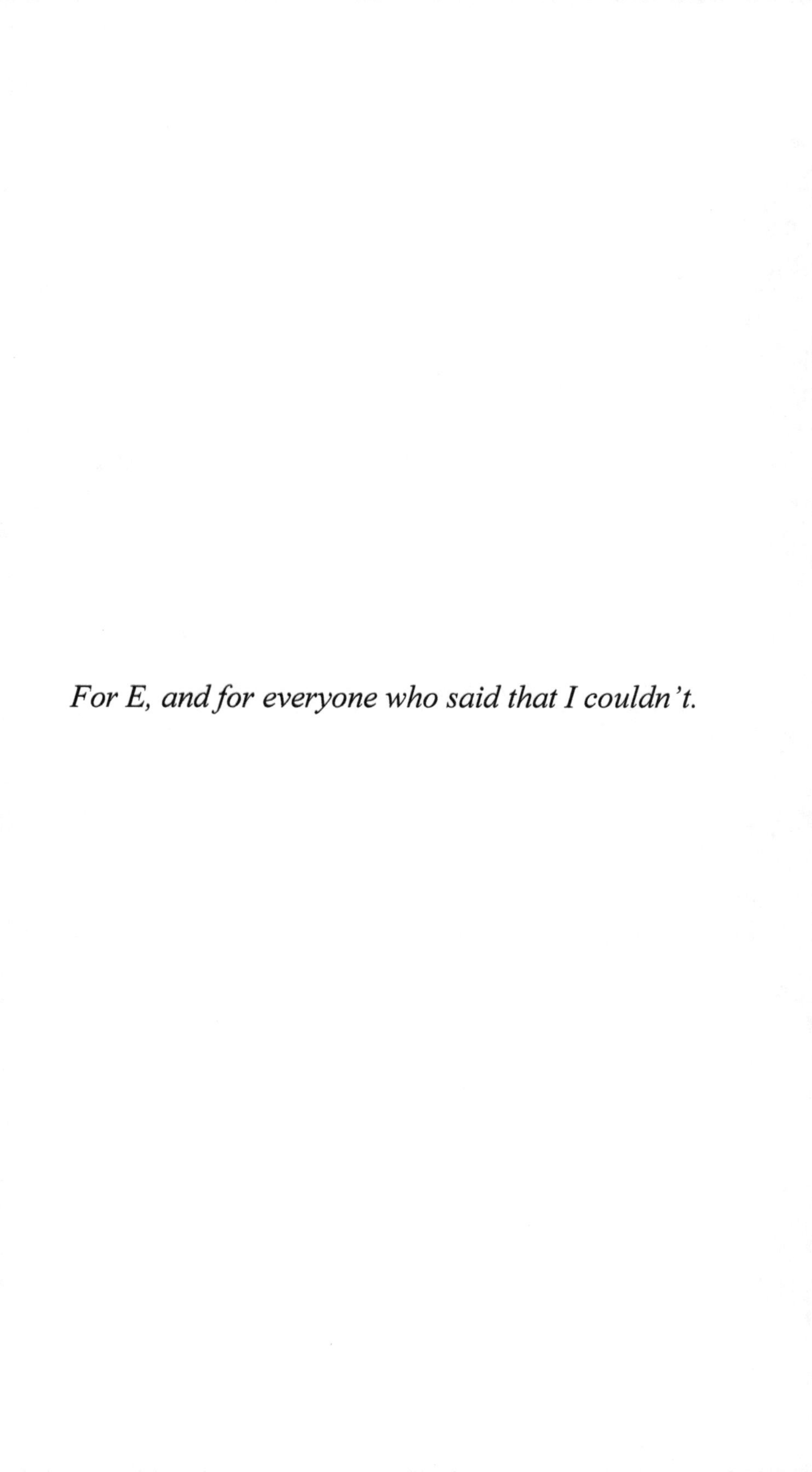

For E, and for everyone who said that I couldn't.

Story Directory

Pyromania

The blaze started just after 1:00 am. A mother and father lay asleep in their bed, blissfully ignorant. Their child – a boy named Jax – was absent from his bedroom.

Unbeknownst to his parents, Jax sat downstairs in the kitchen, toying with a lighter. The flame from his father's 'missing' lighter was the only thing visible in the darkness of the room. Jax put his finger near the flame and burned its tip, and instead of wincing, Jax smiled.

At only nine years old, Jax was fascinated by fire. He loved the vibrancy of its colours, the hues that he identified within its permeation. Jax was also quite fond of the paraphernalia associated with fires, keeping a collection of cheap lighters hidden in the safety of an empty shoebox. But above everything else, Jax was attracted to fire for one reason: the way it made him *feel*.

Fire made Jax feel warm inside. Fire made him feel euphoric, even delirious at times. Jax often had impulses to be closer to the minuscule fires he set in the privacy of his room. This typically resulted in small burns on his fingers and hands, which he skillfully hid from his worrying mother. Though, this night was different. Tonight, Jax would release the burning desire inside him to experience a real fire.

Jax waited until his parents were fast asleep before creeping up the stairs and yielding outside their bedroom door. As always, the door was closed, which was exactly what Jax was counting on. So, Jax squatted on the floor and got to work.

After contemplating where to start his fire, Jax had finally decided on the entrance to his parent's bedroom. Not to harm them, per se. Rather, it was simply one of the only rooms in the whole house that had carpet, making it a prime candidate for catching ablaze.

Having grabbed a lighter and several tea towels from the kitchen, Jax crouched in the hallway and waited. He did not quite know what he was waiting for, but he knew when it was time to act – he could feel it. Jax reached for the rags and stuffed them in the crack between the bedroom door and the ground. Once the crack was filled, he reached for the lighter. Every inch that his hand moved, a quiver struck him.

Then he did it.

It started small, as most fires do. The tea towel farthest to the left was ignited and within seconds, the flames had travelled to the far-right. It was happening. Jax repositioned himself to face the growing fire and observed it. He watched until the fire burnt through tea towels, the sweet smell of smoke burning his nostrils. Jax smiled, eyes still fixated on the flames. He found his hands moving towards the burnt fabric under the crack of the door., and Jax rubbed them together as if he were warming up at a campfire.

From inside his parent's bedroom, Jax heard his father murmur something and began to worry. For a moment, Jax wondered if this had been a mistake.

Could Jax try to extinguish the fire on his own?

Should he call for help?

Ultimately, Jax stayed in his spot on the carpet, his legs crisscrossed like the child that he should have been.

A scream bellowed as Jax's father yelled at his wife to wake up.

“There’s a fire,” yelled Jax’s father. “Jen, wake up for God's sake!”

“Jax!” The sound of Jax’s mother screaming his name filled the room. Then, so did the sound of coughing.

The thickening smoke pouring into their room made their voices horse and evoked bouts of coughing from them both. Jax’s father lunged for the door, but his son was there to halt him from the other side. Jax held onto the door handle with all his might, despite its rising temperature.

“What in the –?” his father yelled in confusion.

Jax heard the desperation in his father’s voice, accompanied by his mother sobbing in the background. Although he did not want to cause his parents harm, Jax could not risk them extinguishing the display of warm colours. It was just too beautiful.

Jax continued to hold the doorknob, not letting the scolding temperature affect him in the slightest. With his father slowly being asphyxiated by the thickening of the smoke, his strength was dwindling. Soon enough, the doorknob stopped jiggling and the despondent cries from inside the room ceased altogether.

The heat was heavenly underneath Jax's sweaty and blistering palms. Whilst his pupils dilated, his body seemed to immobilize itself in the exhilaration of the moment. The fire had now spread to the walls in the hallway where Jax sat, but he had not yet noticed. He was still fixated on that quaint spot underneath the door – the spot that was now engulfed in flames.

The approaching wail of sirens perked Jax's. They pierced closer and closer with each second until finally, they came to a stop. Returning to the reality of the situation, Jax began to panic for the first time all night. He arose quickly before squatting again to pick up the remnants of the burnt towels. Jax swung open the door to his parent's bedroom and threw the tea towels into the flames, destroying the evidence.

Just as quickly as the fire had started, Jax sprinted into his bedroom and catapulted himself into his bed. Despite the fire nearing his quarters, Jax laid underneath his spaceship bed covers, pretending to be fast asleep.

The emergency responder's kicked in the front door, a stampede of footsteps migrated from the porch to the first floor to the second. Jax was promptly discovered and carried to safety.

Outside, medical personnel swarmed around Jax and gave him a thick thermal blanket to shield him from the cold. As he sat in the back of a parked ambulance, Jax was pleased with himself. The firefighters and paramedics asked Jax if he was okay, staring at him sympathetically.

"Poor thing," one of them murmured. "Must be in shock."

"Well, yeah. A fire's traumatizing for an adult, but a child? I can't even imagine what he's going through right now," the other responded.

Traumatizing, they said. Jax deplored that word because the experience hadn't done any such thing to him. Yes, he killed his parents, but it was worth it. This inferno was worth it. And deep down, Jax knew that this was the beginning of something beautiful.

The day had come once again, the anniversary of his parent's deaths. Now thirty-two years old, Jax Stevens had not changed one bit.

The many years that passed had not phased Jax, but rather, tempted him to act again. Ever since that momentous night, he wanted to experience that rush again. Jax knew that he was fortuitous, that he ought to be thankful he was never caught and convicted for the crime. Jax never viewed it as a crime, though. It was more of a sacrifice; something that he *had* to do to get that sweet, satisfactory thrill.

Jax's own home was illuminated by candles at all times of the day. They were in the front hall and the living room, in the dining room and the kitchen. The candles were ubiquitous within Jax's home, occupying every space. They sat on tables, dressers, and even on the floor. Jax had to plot each step he made as to not knock any of the candles down. But sometimes, Jax would overstep and burn the sole of his foot on a flame. It made him feel emotive; it gave him a taste of what he longed for so intensely.

Jax was now in a long-term relationship with a woman named Jillian. After meeting in college, she was infatuated with Jax. Jillian loved playing with Jax's ash-blond hair, and looking into his eyes made her swoon. She had always noticed that Jax was more reserved than most individuals, but she did not mind. Jillian viewed it as shyness, which to her, was an attractive feature

Jillian loved Jax with everything that she had in her – he just set her soul on fire.

Life wasn't always so picturesque, though. Jax's inclination towards fire had become an issue ever since Jillian moved in with him. She felt bombarded by the candles and was in a constant state of perspiration while inside the house. Despite her deep love for Jax, things were beginning to boil over. Jillian had reached her limit, which was exactly why she was sending Jax to therapy.

Jillian had set the appointment up a month before she even proposed the idea to Jax. He declined her at first, an indisputable sign of his stubbornness. But Jillian was just as stubborn and did not abstain from her efforts. Each time she pleaded with him, their argument got progressively more heated until eventually, they were both ready to blow. That was until Jillian gave Jax an ultimatum – go to therapy or lose her for good. As much as Jax adored his fire, his love had been stronger for Jillian.

He reluctantly agreed.

The day had come for Jillian to take Jax to his first therapy session. Jax sat in the passenger's seat fiddling his fingers and picking at his nails. His fingertips were raw and some of his fingers had burns and blisters on them. Whenever he saw Jillian look over at him, he nonchalantly slid his hands into the sleeves of his oversized denim jacket. She saw the blisters anyways and stayed quiet for a moment.

"When do you think it… you know, started?" Jillian asked.

She took turns between keeping her eyes on the road and looking at Jax, but he would not make eye contact with her. Jillian stopped trying. Their car was brimmed with silence until Jax finally answered.

"It never started, Jill," he said softly. "It just always was, you know?" Jax sighed. "I guess you don't know if you're making me go to this God damned place."

Jillian was appalled.

"Oh really," she said. "You're going to go there?" Jillian paused for a brief second to regain her composure, but it did little to aid her. "You're the one who doesn't know anything. You have no idea what it's like watching you be like this, year after year. The number of times I've had to shoo people away from visiting the house is ridiculous. And you know why? It's because I'm embarrassed. I'm embarrassed about the stupid candles and I'm embarrassed by you."

Jillian's words were toxic. She spat them at Jax as if they were venom, and to him, they were. Jax stayed silent, retreating from the conversation. Once Jillian realized that Jax was not going to rebut her, she became quiet as well.

The pair drove in the tangible silence for the remainder of the trip.

The psychological clinic could not have come sooner. When Jillian finally pulled up to the front of the building, she kicked Jax out.

"Out, now." For the first time during the whole trip, Jax looked at his girlfriend. Likewise, Jillian stared at him, looking deeply into the eyes that she had once been so fond of. Those eyes seemed as cold as stone now. "I'll be back in an hour to get you."

Jax turned his back to Jillian and prematurely exited the car before it had even been put into park. Once on the sidewalk, he turned around, this time to face the vehicle. But the car was already speeding off, leaving Jax in its trails.

As expected, the interior of the waiting room was bland and mundane; Jax felt lethargic the moment he entered. There was a broad, wilting plant near the front desk that smelt rotten when Jax went to check-in. Opposite to the plant was a rickety table with a stack of outdated magazines and pre-used crossword puzzles on it. One painting hung on the wall above, a dull illustration of the human brain. Jax eyed the place with disgust. God, would he love to set it ablaze.

"Jax Stevens?"

A woman with rather wide hips waddled into the waiting room. Jax looked up and winced when he saw her. The woman was Lydia Macomb, his new therapist. Lydia accompanied Jax into a side room where her office was located. Lydia's office was almost as bland as the waiting room, except there were spontaneous dashes of pink throughout. Jax would not have minded setting this room ablaze, too.

"Mr. Stevens, have you ever been assessed by a professional regarding your psychological state?" Lydia Macomb asked.

Jax did not answer, as he was preoccupied with conjuring images of what the office would look like if it were burning. Her goliath bookcase would be in an inferno, with each page of every book disintegrating from the heat. He imagined how the plush teddy bear on her desk would burn the quickest, and how the room's abrasive pops of pink would be replaced with pigments of orange.

"Mr. Stevens?"

Jax awoke, saying, "Sorry, I'm just really tired." Lydia's eyes widened and she began writing ferociously in her notebook.

"Interesting," she noted.

The two conversed about Jax's mental well-being. They discussed his childhood and the deaths of his parents, though Jax was careful not to disclose too much information. His therapist instantly latched onto the idea that it was this trauma causing him psychological distress. Jax played into Lydia's conclusions and acted as if it were the tragic death of his parents that began the obsession with fire. Lydia thought of Jax as being the most cooperative and honest patient that she had ever seen. Jax thought of Lydia as the most gullible excuse of a therapist that had ever existed.

They continued chatting back and forth until their time was up. Jax eagerly awaited his dismissal, and the moment that Lydia Macomb sat up from her spinning, leather chair, he vanished. Jax walked quickly into the waiting room and then out of it, making his way to the outside of the building. Jillian was already parked, waiting for him.

Jax slowly made his way to the car, which was stopped a little way up the parking lot. He hopped into the car and Jillian began to drive. Like earlier, Jax and Jillian stayed mute during the car ride home. She did not ask how the session went, which was helpful since Jax did not want to talk about it. He knew that he would just get yelled at again for not taking the meeting seriously. Jax never liked being yelled at. In that respect, he was still a little boy.

For some reason, Jax could not stop thinking about his parents; the people that he had killed. But as much as he pondered and thought, he did not feel remorse. Instead, he wondered if his parents relished in the warmth as they were engulfed in flames. He knew that he sure would.

Jillian turned the corner and her heart sank to her stomach. Looking forward in fear, she saw a cloud of smoke. “Jax,” she stammered.

Jillian pulled over, stopped the car, and pointed forward. Jax’s house, their house, was on fire. Jax’s mouth dropped open and his eyes sparkled – it was a sign. Jillian fumbled in her purse to find her phone and when she did, she called for emergency services with her fingers shaking.

Jillian yelled into the phone, disclosing their address to the operator. Jax did not hear her, though. He was too busy admiring the delicacy of the flames. But it wasn’t enough. They were too far away. Jax wanted to see the fire more clearly, and so he exited the car. Walking towards his house, Jax was in awe.

Noticing his absence, Jillian lunged out of the car to fetch her boyfriend. Jax had already reached the front porch and was starting up the porch.

"Jax! Get back here," Jillian yelled. She went to scream again but choked on a thick cloud of smoke. Jillian tried to move forward to stop him but failed to do so. The smoke was travelling out of the house and into the surrounding area, nearing closer by the second. While the clouds of gray were too powerful for her, Jax savoured in it. He breathed it in as if it were oxygen in his lungs.

The smoke *was* his oxygen.

Their house was now completely engulfed in flames. Jillian cried when she pictured all her belongings burning to pieces inside. She began to weep, but yet again, struggled to do so from the smoke. Her eyes burned and began to water, and her throat began to swell. Jillian clumsily backed herself out of the front yard and away from the density of the smoke, allowing herself to breathe once more.

Onlookers gathered around the scene, and the distant sound of sirens approached the fire. Jillian raised her head to take one last look at the man that she loved, while he himself took one last breath.

With that, Jax opened the burning door and stepped into the inferno.

There's Something in the Shadows

Perfect!" said Betty Davis as she placed the final piece of paper mâché on her homemade pumpkin costume. "I'm going to have the best costume in the whole neighbourhood."

Her mother smiled down at her. It *was* quite an impressive creation for a child of Betty's age. At eleven years old, she was showing an evident interest in the arts. Every chance that Betty got, she was drawing and painting, or thinking about drawing and painting. Oddly enough, Betty had spawned the idea for her pumpkin costume while practicing arithmetic in class. Her creativity never ceased.

When she approached her mother with the idea earlier in the month, Joan Davis was incredibly proud of her eldest daughter. A mere two weeks later, on the evening of October 30th, 1945, Betty's costume was complete. With that, Halloween preparations in the Davis household were in full swing, though such spirit was not present in every family member.

Betty's little sister, Shirley, did not have such a festive disposition. Unlike Betty, Shirley was incredibly shy and feared practically everything around her. In the evening, Shirley was often plagued with night terrors. Joan and her husband, Charles, were at a loss. They simply did not know how to proceed. In an attempt to force their youngest daughter closer to independence, they decided to let Betty and Shirley trick-or-treat alone this year.

Shirley walked into the kitchen to join her mother and sister. Her mother had encouraged Shirley to try on her own costume, and so she did. Shirley thought that she looked ridiculous in such attire; and to think, she wasn't even wearing her wig and makeup yet!

"How precious!" gushed Joan.

Shirley had a frown plastered permanently on her young face. She was not pleased, and she wanted her mother to know it. Joan had known that Shirley was opposed to going out trick-or-treating at all, but it was for the best. Shirley continued to frown.

Betty caught a glimpse of her sister's face and piped in, saying, "Oh, come off it, Shirley. Momma sewed that costume just for you. What's wrong with being a clown?" Betty giggled mischievously.

Shirley's eyes fumed with frustration. Betty always had to give her own opinion, despite it not being relevant. Betty could never just be a sibling. She was not even Shirley's friend. Instead, she was the heroic big sister – a poster child to their parents.

Joan and Charles Davis were not so innocent, either. They often overlooked Shirley and her anxious tendencies, as they did not know what to do with her. Ashamed and confused, they essentially did nothing for the youngest Davis. The couple pretended that Shirley's ailments did not exist and that if they ignored them hard enough, Shirley's fears would vanish.

They never ignored Betty, though. How could they? Their parents would rave to the neighbours about Betty's art projects and her performance in grade school. When asked how Shirley was doing, her parents would simply reply with "Good."

Shirley was only eight years old, though she still knew what favouritism was. She had learned it first-hand, and it scared her. Many things frightened Shirley. The dark, for instance, or creepy crawlers, and unbeknownst to her parents, Shirley had recently adopted another fear – one that stemmed directly from her familial issues. Of course, this was the fear of rejection.

This fear was prominent in Shirley's mind as she stood at the entryway to the kitchen. She eagerly awaited her mother's response. Joan looked at both of her daughters in a back-and-forth motion, her eyes finally landing on Shirley.

"Sweetie, I know this is out of your comfort zone. But sometimes, you must do things that you do not want to do," her mother replied smoothly, soon adding, "I did put a lot of effort into that costume of yours."

While looking down at the clown suit, Shirley concluded that she did hate it. She did not like the itching that the plush, white collar induced, nor was she a fan of the red pom-poms lining vertically down her torso. She thought about what the full costume would look like when she went out with Betty the following night. Her sister would look great, and Shirley would look like a fool, as per usual.

Shirley turned on a dime and stomped out of the room, hearing her mother sigh loudly behind her. Her stomps took her up the stairs, though she was careful not to make too much noise. After all, she did not want to get into any more trouble.

Once in her bedroom, Shirley tucked herself into bed and tried to push away her negative thoughts. Her brain was crowded and her mind tangled. It was a spider's web, a chaotic labyrinth.

Just as Shirley was beginning to settle down, the door creaked open, and Betty walked in. Creeping into the bedroom, Betty took a seat on the edge of her little sister's bed, careful not to wake her. In a slew of boredom, Betty took a moment to inspect the bedroom that they shared.

The room was lacking any illumination, though Betty could still detect the faint colour of their pale-yellow wallpaper. She waited until her eyes had fully adjusted to the dark before viewing them any further. When ready, her eyes moved around the walls until she spotted some of her artistic creations. They were stuck to the wall, a gallery of her own.

To Betty's surprise, Shirley sat up in bed and stared at her sister. Betty took note of the disinterest on Shirley's face and considered that her sister must be very upset. She spoke anyways.

"Why do you have to be like that to mom?" she had asked.

"I'm not anything to her," Shirley snapped.

Betty skipped a beat before speaking next. "Well, I wanted to tell you some things about Halloween, Shirley. You know, make sure that you understand the plan."

Betty spoke to Shirley as her superior, not her sister. The way she spoke was patronizing to Shirley, and so she ignored Betty.

Irritated by Shirley's lack of attention, Betty talked a bit louder and her tone nonchalant. "*AS* you know, mom and dad asked if I could take you out for Halloween alone this year – just us. And being the greatest big sister there is, I agreed. You best be behaving tomorrow night, Shirley, because I won't put up with any nonsense. None of your crying or whining."

Shirley sat in her bed, dumbfounded at Betty's condescending lecture. She looked at Betty with eyes wide open and a blank expression, until finally, she departed. Betty said goodnight to her sister as she hopped off of Shirley's bed and maneuvered swiftly into her own.

Within minutes, Betty was fast asleep, dreaming of whatever she usually dreamed about. Perhaps her dreams were filled with the prospect of becoming a famous painter; perhaps she dreamt of colours.

Shirley, on the other hand, was not so fortunate. After an hour or so of trying to fall asleep, Shirley eventually succeeded. However, her dreams were not so picturesque. She did not dream of her future or vibrancy. That night, Shirley dreamt of black.

The next evening, Joan Davis stepped back to look at her children. On the left was Betty dressed in black trousers and an orange top; the paper mâché pumpkin sat atop her head. The pumpkin had two little eye holes poked out for Betty to see, as well as an opening in the mouth for her to breathe. Inside the pumpkin head, it was a tad dark, but Betty was beaming despite this.

To the right was little Shirley, dressed head to toe in her clown costume. Her face had been done up by her mother. Shirley's skin was painted a ghastly white and the entirety of her button nose was coloured red. A roughly shaped triangle had been placed above and below each of Shirley's eyes. To culminate the outfit was a coiled red wig that matched her round red nose. Shirley deemed the costume to be hideous.

At that moment, Betty and Shirley's father entered the room to view his daughters. He eyed them up and down and then turned in the direction of his wife.

"The girls look wonderful," he said with a smile.

"They certainly do look great," Joan replied, "I cannot believe how well Betty's costume turned out."

Annoyed with Betty's attention, Shirley spoke out, saying, "Can we go now?" Her parents chuckled and proceeded to shoo them out the door, bidding them farewell.

Betty waited until their front door shut before she started marching towards the nearest house. She did not wait for Shirley. It was obvious that Betty took her candy acquisition very seriously.

"Hey," Shirley panted, "Wait up!" She tried to catch up to Betty but struggled to do so in her clown costume. A few beads of sweat were appearing on her made-up face, causing the colours to blur together.

Once Betty stopped in front of a house nearby, Shirley was finally able to meet with her sister. She paused to regain her breath while evaluating the home in front of her. Why Betty chose this house, Shirley did not know. There was nothing special about the home; it looked as mundane as the rest of their neighbourhood.

Suddenly, the front door flung open and a girl around Betty's age walked outside. She was dressed as a witch and wearing a long black cloak. Her dark, pointed hat contrasted her blonde hair; a fake mole decorated her face. The girl was Margaret May.

Margaret was Betty's best friend from school, and they had known each other since the first grade. Many a times had she been over to the Davis's house before. Shirley was not particularly a fan of Margaret, as was the norm with most of Betty's companions.

For Shirley, the night dragged on and on; it was an incredibly tedious affair. The three girls made their way through the entirety of the neighbourhood, collecting enough candy to last them for weeks. Although Shirley made a noble attempt to continue holding her heavy pale of candy, the night had tired her out immensely. She complained to Betty.

"Just one more house," Betty had said to Shirley. Too exhausted to dispute her sister, Shirley decided to stay behind.

"Alrighty, stay put. We'll be right back," said Betty. She gave her sister an intense look as she and Margaret walked away.

A minute passed; then two, and then three. Betty and Margaret had still not returned. Shirley had followed their instructions to stay put and had not moved from her spot on the curb. It seemed to be getting darker by the second, and Shirley was beginning to feel uneasy. She pushed the feeling away, only for it to creep up on her once more.

She waited and waited until she had lost her patience. Shirley was cold and scared, and she just wanted to go home. A tear rolled down Shirley's cheek.

The sky had darkened, and the streets had now emptied – not a child or parent was in sight. Shirley made up her mind to get up from the curb, and so she started up the road to find Betty and Margaret. This street was incredibly quiet, the only sound being the clicking of Shirley's shoes, echoing against the pavement.

There were far and few light posts to illuminate Shirley's path. To remedy this, she moved her little feet quickly to get from post to post. It did little to help, as once Shirley got to the light, she hesitated to leave it. At this rate, she would never catch up to them.

Shirley shakily looked ahead to the next light post to gauge the distance from her current position. While turning her head, she saw something odd – another light. It was faint, though visibly present in the sea of darkness. The light was the same colour as the pale-yellow wallpaper in her bedroom, and it made her feel warm inside. As Shirley wondered what it was, she lost herself in the light. Her eyes became locked, and she was unable to look away. Shirley continued to stare in a reverie she did not ever want to abandon.

Soon enough, the staring did not suffice, and Shirley wanted to touch the little light. She began walking towards it, which meant leaving the safety of the streetlamp. Though this time, she did not care. Shirley felt euphoric; the little glow illuminated the darkness inside of her. In an instant, the anxieties that had plagued Shirley disappeared. She had no fears as she distanced herself from the streetlamp.

Just a little way up the road was Betty and Margaret, having lost track of time while visiting more houses. Their carelessness quickly multiplied their stops until finally, they had visited a dozen houses. Only when they were tired enough themselves did they finally make their way back to Shirley. As they neared the spot where they had left Shirley, Betty stopped in her tracks, causing Margaret to collide with her.

"What?" Margaret had asked with attitude.

"Look," replied Betty. "What's she doing?"

The two girls stood confused and terrified. They too saw the light, and they witnessed Shirley's slow movements towards it. This glow was floating in the dark brush of the forest, which was adjacent to the road. It began to move steadily towards the street – towards Shirley – and stopped promptly before a streetlamp.

Betty hollered to Shirley and received no reply. Shirley continued to trudge towards the light until she paused, also stopping underneath the streetlamp. She stared as the light diminished and a hand reached out from the dark, prompting Shirley to drop her bucket of candy. Seconds later, Shirley reached her own hand into the darkness to make contact with the stranger. The moment their hands grasped, Betty and Margaret barreled down the street.

The girls could see a vague outline of the figure holding Shirley's hand. They were tall, lean, and unproportionate to that of a human. With their free hand, the stranger set the light – evidently from a lamp – down on the ground, allowing Betty and Margaret to catch a glimpse. The hand was mangled and so pale, it was as if all the blood had left their body. Their fingers were long, and their nails chipped; Betty and Margaret never knew that a hand could look so horrific.

In a single movement, the figure gestured for Shirley to follow them; they loomed over Shirley and waited. The stranger started to walk backwards and with ease, she followed the figure towards the dark. The abyss swallowed the pair and just like that, little Shirley

Davis disappeared into the shadows, leaving behind nothing more than a spilt pale of candy.

Why Don't You Cry?

The summer after Wren turned 12, her father dropped a propane tank on his foot.

He had been carrying it out from their backyard shed, lazily transferring it to the deck. For one reason or another, Wren's father lost his grip. Flip-flops proved to be a poor choice of footwear because the edge of the propane tank plunged into bone and flesh; there was no cushioning to lessen the blow.

When it happened, Wren's mother was in the kitchen, and Wren herself was watching a cheesy film from the 1980s. She did not see what happened when her father stumbled in through the sliding door, but she heard her mother's reaction.

"Oh my God, what happened? What did you do?"

Heavy footsteps echoed through the house and into Wren's ears.

"I had a little accident," was Wren's father's response. "It's fine, I'm fine. It's just a cut."

Wren wandered downstairs, curious as to what had happened. Once she entered the family room, there was no need to inquire for any specifics – seeing the blood was enough for her. A trail of it had trickled onto the floor, a path of crimson red dotting the hardwood from the back door to the family room. The trail ended in front of the couch, where Wren's father was slouched on the cushion, holding a white towel to his right foot.

Make that a red towel.

The fabric was drenched in blood with little left of its original stark white. When Wren's father removed the towel to assess the damage, Wren bore a look of confusion. His big toe was almost severed, and the wound was gushing blood, but her father's face did not show an inkling of pain.

"Does it hurt?" Wren asked her father.

Straightening his posture, he responded with, “Not really. It looks worse than it is.”

Wren did not understand how her father could be so nonchalant with his toe hanging from his foot like a door hinge; a door about to come *off* its hinge.

The room was still, except for the continuous flow of blood. Wren’s mother broke the silence, saying, “Come on, we’re going to the emergency room.”

“I don't need to go to the hospital. It doesn't hurt that bad, look.” Wren’s father arose defensively, and Wren caught a wince that flashed across his face.

Her mother persisted. “Look at your foot. That needs stitches, I don't care how much it does or doesn't hurt. It’ll get infected if you leave it.”

“Just get me a bandage and some ointment and I’ll be fine.”

They went back and forth for 15 minutes until Wren’s father conceded. As her parents departed for the hospital, Wren’s father gave a jovial thumbs-up. Wren was not quite sure how to respond. When her parents arrived home a few hours later, Wren's father's toe was stitched back together. The doctor told him that he was lucky and that he should take it easy.

Her father was back at work the next day.

About a year later, Wren's father came home from an adult league baseball game. He played weekly that summer, and many summers before it, every game an evening game. Her father always came home around 10:30 pm, since the diamond was a fair drive from home. Wren had been downstairs watching TV, her mother already in bed, when her father came home. Wren's father set his keys down and greeted her with a "Hey, pal." A casual hello, as if nothing were wrong. Only, something *was* wrong.

"What happened to your nose?" Wren asked him.

"Oh, just caught a ball to the face. All the guys said it looks broken, but it doesn't feel too bad. The pitcher felt like crap, though." He chuckled.

Wren ignored her father's assertion. "And you drove home with a broken nose?"

“Well, yeah. But I’m alright. I picked up some food on the way back. Your burger and fries are on the front table.”

Wren turned her head and sure enough, a cheeseburger meal was waiting for her. Her father had picked up fast food after driving an hour home with a broken nose, and he saw nothing wrong with it. Wren was baffled.

“Are you going to go to a doctor for that?” It was a stupid question.

“No, it's okay. I’ll be fine.” With an exaggerated sigh, her father sank into the recliner and pulled out his cellphone.

“Does it hurt?”

“It's a little uncomfortable.”

“But does it hurt?”

“Not really.”

Unlike with the propane incident, Wren’s father could not be swayed to go to the hospital. So, she said goodnight and went upstairs. Though once Wren was in bed, she could not fall asleep. She just laid in the dark, stared at the ceiling, and wondered why her father did not cry. Strong and dependable, Wren's father was someone whom she had always looked up to, someone she wanted to emulate. The last thought that crossed Wren's mind as she drifted to sleep was that perhaps she should not cry, either.

The summer ended, and Wren started the eighth grade that September. Sometime after that, she asked her mother a question as she was being driven home from school.

"Has dad ever cried?"

Her mother laughed nervously. "I've only ever seen him cry twice. Once when you were born and once when your grandfather died."

"Does he get sad?"

"If he does, he doesn't show it."

Wren had never seen her father cry. On the other hand, Wren had seen her mother cry plenty of times. Her father was a brick wall, while her mother was an empath, crying often. Wren's mother cried when she dropped her daughter off for the first day of kindergarten, and she teared up when Wren had her first piano recital. Wren's mother even cried a bit when she broke a finger. Injured or not, she was always willing to show how she was feeling. Yet, no matter how injured Wren's father was, he did not shed a tear.

Later that year, Wren joined her school's Skiing and Snowboarding Club. Despite both her parents being skiers, Wren chose snowboarding, and for the most part, she excelled at it. On one of their last outings to the ski hill, Wren decided to pursue an advanced slope.

Her ride was enjoyable until the hill got steeper, and then, it was not.

Wren lost her balance and fell forward, her body doing somersaults down the hill, and her snowboard binding still attached to one foot. After she lost momentum, Wren laid like a ragdoll on the snow. That was when the pain began.

All at once, the wrist of her right hand stung and throbbed and burned. Some skiers came down the hill and asked if Wren was alright, but she did not respond. One of them left to get first aid, while the other stayed with Wren. She sat on the ground with Wren and talked, but all Wren heard was white noise. She wanted to cry but could not let herself do it in front of some stranger, and so, she left her face blank.

The medical snowmobile drove Wren down the remainder of the hill, amber lights flashing. In the lodge, the medic asked Wren questions and examined her injured wrist, bending it up and down. It hurt like hell, but she did not tell him that. Wren did not say it was excruciating when he rotated her hand like that, or that it swelled with pain even when he touched it. The medic wrapped it in gauze and informed Wren's teachers of what had happened.

Upon the bus's return to school, a teacher stayed with Wren until they found her mother waiting in the parking lot. They discussed what had happened, and the teacher relayed what the medic had said:

"She doesn't seem to be in much pain, but I would take her to the hospital, just in case."

Wren's mother did as the medic and teacher advised, promptly taking her daughter to the emergency room. After an hour-long wait and two x-rays, the E.R. doctor determined that Wren had a severe fracture that bordered a break. The doctor counted to three and snapped Wren's wrist, a clean break. Wren's mother cried at the snap of bone.

On the ride home, Wren stared at her new cast and felt a disconnect.

"How are you feeling?" Wren's mother asked.

"I'm fine," Wren asserted.

Her mother was driving and had to keep her eyes on the road, but Wren still saw her face. Wren's mother looked defeated, sadness swelling in her eyes. Wren felt a pang of guilt but did not know why. It made her feel sad, even, but it did not make her sad enough to cry.

Wren's father gave her a hug when she and her mother arrived home and was the first to sign the cast.

"It might be annoying at first, but the cast won't be for long," he told Wren. "Does it hurt?"

"Nope, not really. I didn't even cry."

"That's my girl. What a trouper, you are."

Looking at her father with emulation in her eyes, Wren smiled.

Ostinato

Violet Matheson played with passion, and a little too much of it. Her fingers moved both ferociously and elegantly across the strings of her violin, blisters forming in the process.

She practiced in her high school's auditorium every day after classes had concluded. The room had an echo that made her already forceful music sound even more powerful. As per the norm, Violet stood in the center of the stage, performing a sonata. Every stroke of her bow rang loudly on the instrument's body, and she could feel the vibrations in her heart. The auditorium was silent aside from the intense melodies exerted from the violin. In the heart of the large room, Violet was all alone. From time to time, she would change her gaze from her finger placement to the sea of empty seats in front of her. Such seats could easily fit a couple hundred people.

Sometimes Violet would imagine each seat filled with an adoring audience member, every one of them listening to her in awe. She smiled. Violet was eager for the day when this fantasy would become a reality. Her acceptance into the Burckland School of Music would be the catalyst for her dream of being a professional musician.

This had been her goal ever since Violet had taken lessons as a young girl. Once she had entered high school, Violet thrived in her practice. The auditorium was free to use by any student if they signed their name on a sheet and cleaned up after themselves. Luckily, Violet was the only one to ever use the room, as there were few other students interested in the performing arts. This was undoubtedly due to a lack of funding for the school's arts program. Beaten up guitars and stained sheet music filled the music program's classroom. Even worse, Violet was almost certain that no one had ever cleaned the spit valves for the trombones. The very thought made her cringe.

Violet strung her last note harshly, concluding the piece with zest. The note echoed off every sound-proofed wall in the room, ringing in Violet's ears. When the ringing ceased, she heard an unfamiliar noise – clapping. The claps sounded eerie in the emptiness of the room. Unlike her music, Violet did not like how this sound echoed.

She looked around the room and saw another student walk down the middle of the aisle leading to the stage. He wore a t-shirt with a musical joke written on it. It read: *WHAT DO YOU GET WHEN A PIANO FALLS DOWN A MINE SHAFT? A FLAT MINOR.* Violet hid a chuckle.

"Wow," the boy said as he reached the stage, "that was amazing."

"Thanks," Violet said shyly. There was an awkward pause. Despite her fierce performances, Violet was a timid girl and had no friends. She fidgeted with her fingers, waiting for him to say something.

"I'm Zayne." Another pause.

"I'm Violet. I haven't seen you here before."

"I just transferred for the rest of my senior year. Pretty shitty, huh?" Zayne smiled.

Violet nodded her head and there was silence once more. She took this time to examine the boy. He had short, wavy hair that was not quite red; it was an auburn. His boyish smile was unlike anything she had ever experienced before.

"Your music is great. How long have you been playing for?"

"About ten years," she replied.

"Do you want to do anything with it? You know, the violin." Zayne looked at her with genuine interest.

"Yeah, I really want to go to Burckland for their Bachelor of Music program."

"Oh," he said, "you would totally be able to do that. You're so talented, Violet."

"I think I'll be able to get in." She paused. The confidence was momentary and Violet reverted back to into submission. "I hope so, anyways."

"You know, I play the piano. I would love to help you practice, sometime. Maybe play a duet. Only if you want, though." The moment was surreal to Violet.

"I'd love that," she said. "Thanks."

It was a Friday afternoon, and the evening was nearing closer. They packed up to go home and decided to meet in the auditorium Mondays and Wednesdays after classes were over. Violet was giddy as Zayne left the auditorium that evening. The widest smile Violet ever had accompanied her on the walk home.

Over the weekend, Violet waited eagerly to see Zayne again. She sifted through the mound of sheet music in her bedroom to find a piece by her favorite composer – a serenade. She practiced it over and over until her parents yelled at her to stop. But Violet was not only waiting to see her crush again; she was waiting to hear back from Burckland. The end of January was approaching, which meant that the admissions decisions would be sent out soon. Violet was thrilled at the prospect of receiving an acceptance. She was desperate to make her dream a reality.

Monday rolled around and Violet could barely contain her excitement. She was in the auditorium at 2:30pm sharp. To prepare for their meeting, Violet had pulled her silky, black hair into a tight bun and she had put on mascara. Violet never paid much attention to what she looked like, though that had all changed now. She wanted to look pretty for Zayne. Suddenly, Violet worried that her appearance was not enough, and so she altered her school uniform, hiking her kilt and lowering her knee-high socks. Violet was smoothing her kilt out when she saw him approach and beamed when Zayne walked through the doors.

"Hey," he said.

"Hey." Yet again, an awkward pause ensued. Violet hoped that Zayne would say something about the way that she looked. She waited.

"Let's get to work, shall we?"

Violet's hopes dropped as the pair walked up the steps that led to the stage. A rickety acoustic piano was now in the center, having been moved out of storage for their practice. It was rougher than Violet imagined, and she wondered if the keys would stick.

"What did you want to play?" asked Zayne. Violet pulled out a folder from her backpack and handed it to him with a child's excitement.

She smiled shyly and started unpacking her violin from its case. "I really like this piece," Violet said. "It's the one that I played when I auditioned for Burckland. I've probably done it a hundred times and that still isn't enough." She chuckled.

"I bet you did great."

Violet blushed. Throughout her whole life, she had never felt so animated around another person. "I'm ready when you are," she said, looking longingly at Zayne.

He walked over to the piano. "Do you mind if I do a warm-up?"

"Not at all."

Violet watched admirably as his fingers ignited the keys, giving the withering piano a life once more. The music was simultaneously melancholy and beautiful. He glided effortlessly from one note to the next, not even looking at where his fingers were going. The pensive music nearly induced tears in Violet's eyes.

Zayne concluded the song and proceeded to casually place Violet's sheet music on the piano's stand. He studied it. His brows furrowed as he focused closely on each note's articulation. "Okay," he said. "I'm all good to go."

"Sounds good," Violet said.

She readied the violin, placing her chin upon the chin rest. She tried not to let her nerves get to her, but she was failing. Violet wanted so desperately to perform well for Zayne that she began to scold herself at the thought of failure. She needed to hear that wonderful validation from him once more. Violet took a deep breath and began.

Zayne played the song's introduction, which was solely the piano. He played on his own for a couple bars before Violet joined in. Once the two instruments met, the sounds that ensued were magical. Each instrument complimented the other, as did the people who played them; they worked together in a delicate harmony. Violet thought of how *right* the moment felt, and even wondered about the prospect of having Zayne as her boyfriend. That would almost be as amazing as Berkley.

At that moment, she faltered. Violet overshot where she was to put her index finger, producing a note that was too sharp. The melody broke.

"What the hell?" The voice was loud and dominating. It did not sound like Zayne.

Violet turned around to face Zayne and the piano. Violet looked at him, her heart having sunk to her stomach. "I'm sorry," she said with a whimper.

"You should be," he said with animosity. A moment later, his voice softened, as did his face. "Let's do it again."

The song played once more, both Violet and Zayne performing their respective parts. To Violet's dismay, the mistake happened again, this time earlier in the piece. Her nerves had consumed her, and she felt miserable for it. She was a disappointment to herself and to Zayne. How could she be such a failure, after all these years of practice?

Out of nowhere, Zayne spoke. "I assume you know what ostinato means." His voice boomed and echoed as loud as their music did.

"It's a phrase," Violet said. She spoke so softly that the sentence almost came out as a whisper. "The persistent repetition of a musical phrase."

"Exactly. Now, use that. Practice again and again. Do it until its perfect." He walked over to Violet but did not face her. "After seeing you perform these past few days, I know what your weakness is. Its your confidence. And as it is, you'll never make it at Burckland. You won't make it anywhere."

That last sentence stung, and Violet felt an intense twinge that occurred in every nerve of her body, all at once. Thoughts of self-deprecation filled her mind, but before the thoughts had time to ruminate, Zayne had already started to pack up.

"I'm going to head out."

Violet did not think her heart could break anymore, but it did. He was leaving and it was her fault. "Oh, alright then."

"Alright, I'll see you Wednesday, then."

Violet nodded her head. Zayne hopped off the stage and walked through the aisle to reach the exit. Once he had left and the doors had shut, Violet began to cry. She cried and cried until her entire being was filled with sorrow, and there were no tears left to shed.

Wednesday had arrived slowly. Violet did not know if she anticipated her next meeting with Zayne or feared it; she pondered this as she waited for him in the auditorium. Violet had prepared for the encounter regardless, her fingers still sore from a round of practice earlier that day.

Zayne arrived punctually and hopped onto the stage, sitting next to Violet. "How's Burckland coming?" he asked enthusiastically.

"It's not," Violet snapped. Zayne looked at her, evidently shocked by her tone. She corrected herself quickly, saying "Sorry."

"It's fine. So, you haven't heard anything back yet?"

"Nope."

"How often do you check your email? It could come any minute now. You should check it again, before we start up practice. We don't want to miss any good news." The idea made Violet uneasy.

"Maybe not right now," she said with a nervous laugh.

"Do it."

Violet stared at her feet before she reluctantly pulled out her cell phone. With wavering fingers, she signed into her email and audibly gasped. It was there – the email was there. In a moment of pure adrenaline, she opened the message and immediately regretted it. The email was a rejection letter. Violet did not know what to say, nor did she know what to do. She internally panicked as she felt her throat close in. It was becoming more difficult to inhale, as if she had forgotten how to breathe. She was drowning in her disgrace.

"Pick up the violin," spat Zayne bitterly.

Violet stayed frozen on the stage floor. When she failed to follow his instructions, Zayne became angry and yelled at her to get up. Only then, did Violet do what she was told. Once they were both standing, Zayne spoke again. "Play our song from Monday. Play it straight through, with no errors. Show me that you aren't really a failure. Prove it."

Robotically, Violet raised the violin to her chin and began to play. Her bowing arm was wobbly with every stroke and her fingers occasionally slipped from the sweat. The first time that this occurred, Zayne barked at her.

"*Ostinato*! Again, again!" Violet began to play once more, though she faulted almost immediately. "I thought you were great, but you're really just terrible. How did either of us think that you would ever be accepted to a school like Burckland?" Violet played the wrong note upon hearing his negativity. Zayne ordered her to play again, and again, and again.

Eventually, Violet had tuned Zayne out so that all she heard was the screeching of her music. The finger placements were wrong, as well as the bow strokes; but she kept going, repeating her mistakes in an indefinite loop. She was digging her fingertips into the strings with so much pressure that she began to bleed. Thoughts of Burckland flooded her mind, followed by the tangibility of her failure. Tears streamed down her cheeks, but she did not stop playing. Her eyes stayed glued on Zayne, across the stage. He looked at her wickedly.

Mrs. Winters, a teacher who had stayed past the bell to mark a stack of tests, heard awful noises coming from the auditorium. Although the walls were meant to be soundproof, she heard faint screeching noises and went in to investigate.

Violet did not hear the teacher walk in, nor did she realize that she was being called. Walking closer to the stage, Mrs. Winters waved her hands around in the air, hoping to catch Violet's attention. It did not work. When Violet finally did stop playing, she dropped the violin on the stage floor, abandoning it in midair. She began to sob.

Mrs. Winters wondered to herself why this student was playing the violin so intensely. "Are you alright?" she asked. Again, Violet did not acknowledge the teacher and instead looked at Zayne. He stared back at her furiously.

While examining the scene, Mrs. Winters took notice of the blood on Violet's hands. It was not much, but in an educational institution such as this, any injury was enough to warrant medical attention. Mrs. Winters departed to fetch the school's nurse at once. After reaching the exit, Mrs. Winters turned around to view the room one last time. Being raised above the remainder of the space, the auditorium look gargantuan from where she was standing. Mrs.

Winters gazed down at Violet as she left the room, observing as she rocked in fetal position on the stage floor. She saw that Violet's eyes were fixated on a spot across the stage. Mrs. Winters could not fathom why she would be staring at an empty spot so profoundly. Mrs. Winters left feeling pitiful and confused.

Down on the stage, Violet was in hysterics. She was a failure. She had always been a failure. She would always be a failure.

"I'm sorry," Violet whispered hoarsely. She stared at Zayne feeling pain in every ounce of her being.

"You should be," he said with spite.

Bird Boy

Holden Michaels does not like the country life. A week after moving from his family's apartment in the city to a rural town a few provinces over, Holden had not assimilated – he simply did not want to.

Although he and his mother had moved into a larger house, Holden missed the sleek, urban interior of their old condo. Even worse, he missed the near-panoramic view of the city that he had from his bedroom window. All he could see now were fields of wheat and the ill-paved street in front of his house; it may as well have been a dirt road.

On the morning of his first day at the new school, Holden was sour. "No smiles for your first day?" his mother asked as she poured cereal into Holden's bowl. His displeased expression did not falter.

"Whatever you say," sulked Holden. His mother fetched the milk and added that to his cereal. He ate it with a frown, exaggerating every crunch. Sitting at their new *plain* table in their new *plain* kitchen, Holden scoffed. He could not believe that he had to reside in such a dump; Holden resented his mother for it.

Having just been left by her husband for a younger woman in her twenties, Holden's mother, Ruth, was devastated. As such, she did what was appropriate for any women to do after experiencing heartbreak; uproot her life to begin a new one. On a single income, they could no longer afford the luxurious lifestyle that they had previously relished in. Funded by the man that abandoned them, Holden and his mother were in financial ruin. Consequently, Ruth made the decision to move herself and Holden to a different province. It was a place where they could start over; a place where she could raise her son properly. At least, that was what she told herself.

Ruth wanted to believe that she was much happier in this older, humble home. She wanted so badly for herself and her son to adjust to their new life. More than anything, she wanted to hate Holden's father. Wealthy, attractive, and a great parent, he was the epitome of her dream husband – or so she thought. Leaving without notice or a goodbye, Ruth and Holden were devastated. Despite all this, Ruth knew that she still loved and missed him, especially his strong hugs and dark brown eyes. Even after all he had done, Ruth wanted him back, which Holden did not understand or support.

After barely eating his cereal, Holden's mother handed him his brand-name backpack and walked him to the porch. To Ruth's pleasurable surprise, the Greenwich Elementary School bus had a stop just up the road from their new home. From what Holden was told, Greenwich was a quaint school with a population of only 112 students.

Holden saw that the bus, which was an obnoxious yellow, had rust spread over its body and that even from afar, the bus emitted chaos. One of its windows was slid down and a small foot was dangling outside of it. Once the bus came to a complete stop, the vehicle jolted, forcing the child's foot back inside.

"Well?" his mother asked with a false tone of enthusiasm. "Are you ready, sport?"

Holden shrugged his shoulders and proceeded to the school bus. He moved his feet slowly, trudging through the dirt, until he got to the doors. The bus driver, an older fellow, was there to greet him.

"Hi there, young man." He smiled a toothless smile. "Hop aboard."

Holden held in a cringe that was sure to have manifested in the form of a skewed face. As he stepped onto the bus, Holden's nostrils flared at the smell of sweat and bubble-gum. Somehow, he thought that the bus was even more repulsive than the house he had just moved into. The smell ceased to dissipate once the bus started moving and Holden had taken his seat. He sat by himself, alone at the very back of the vehicle. Children had stared at Holden as he walked quickly through the middle of the bus with his head down.

"Look at his jeans," whispered one girl with a sloppy ponytail.

Her pig-nosed friend gawked at Holden's expensive pants. They had clean-cut rips, which were intentional for their design, and were dark blue in color. Pig-nose looked down at her own hand-me-down jeans and felt inferior. They had a single, frayed rip in the knee and a few mud stains throughout; nothing compared to the new kid, who was a literal *fancy-pants*.

Even after sitting down on the grimy seat cushion, Holden felt a dozen pairs of eyes on him. He sighed. He could hear whispers about him from across the bus, ranging in topics from his appearance to where in the world he must have come from. Holden did not like being the new kid, nor did he like being an outsider. Back in the city, he had plenty of friends. More specifically, he had a special group of boys that he was chummy with. They used to sit on the school benches every recess, picking on other students and admiring a limited selection of the grade eight girls.

Looking around the bus and at his new peers, Holden winced in disgust. He was in disbelief that these were the people he would be spending the rest of his school days with. He knew that his father would have hated them, too. For a moment, Holden's heart filled with fear. He recognized the already evident divergence between himself and the rest of the children on the bus and wondered if he would make any friends at all. He quickly shooed the thought away, turning his body to look out the window.

Outside, the bus was passing a thick, browning cornfield that contrasted the vibrancy of the sky. The sun shone bright and a few birds flew high above. Holden had never seen a sky so blue, perhaps because it had been so polluted back in the city. The sight was admittedly picturesque, though Holden could not bring himself to come to terms with this truth or his new circumstances. Scenic views do not make this move okay; they do not make his father leaving okay.

"Hey, buddy. How are ya' doing?"

Without hesitation, Holden pretended that he did not hear the boy who spoke. He continued to stare out of the window and silently scolded himself for not having put his earbuds in.

The boy, who happened to have an obnoxiously southern accent, spoke once more. "Buddy? You alright in there?" He chuckled to himself, a few more boys laughing from a few bus seats over.

Holden figured he ought to turn around if there were multiple people laughing at him, for fear of making a poor impression. Who was he kidding; no matter the impression he gave, Holden would always be cast above these petty children. He shifted his body towards the boy. The speaker behind the unpleasant voice was pale and freckled and had brown eyes that reminded Holden of mud. Fitting.

"Hi," said Holden cautiously. The boy was now sitting on Holden's seat, a little too close for his liking. Holden saw that a few other boys were looming around him in the surrounding bus seats.

The speaker's eyes sparkled with enthusiasm. "You from 'round here? Can't say I've seen you before."

"Obviously not," Holden retorted. The boy looked at Holden with distaste.

"Sheesh, sorry I asked."

The boy turned around and made a face to his friends in the neighboring bus seats. When Holden saw the boy beginning to depart from the seat, he panicked. Maybe he did want a friend, a distraction from all that was happening around him.

"Wait," he exclaimed with authority. Holden spoke the word as if it were an order, not a plea. The boy halted and sat down again, facing Holden once more. "Sorry."

"Oh, I'm just pulling your leg," the boy responded lightly. Seeing the negativity on Holden's face, he spoke again, attempting to continue their introduction. "I'm Petey, and this over here is Drew and Harry." He pointed to the two boys in the next bus seat.

"I'm Holden."

"Cool." There was an awkward pause, though it was filled with noise from the other children on the bus. "So," Petey said, "where'd you come from anyways?"

"Toronto," responded Holden. In unison, Petey and the other boys gasped. They had never met a bigshot from Toronto before and were shocked that he had moved to such a small town. Harry looked at Petey, his eyebrows completely raised, and motioned him to inquire further.

Petey spoke once more. “That’s pretty awesome. What did ya’ do for fun in the city?” The three boys stared at Holden, eager to hear about his experiences.

“I don’t know.” Holden spoke with a stagnant pitch as a wave of shyness hit him again. “Video games, I guess.”

The excitement in Petey’s face quickly vanished. With the arrival of yet another unpleasant pause, Holden gave up on the conversation and shifted his body back towards the window. Next to him, Holden could hear whispers spoken with a sense of urgency.

“Alrighty. We talked ‘bout it and we thought we ought to invite ya’ to the creek today.” Holden did not recognize the voice, as it was not Petey who had spoken. He hesitantly turned around. “What?” Holden asked irritably.

“Stoney Creek,” the voice repeated. Holden saw that it was Harry who had spoken. “It’s where we go when we ain’t feeling school.”

"Yeah. We just hang out, skip some stones on the water, do some shootin'. That sorta stuff," chimed Drew.

Holden thought for a moment, turning the proposal over in his mind. "And you don't get caught doing that?"

"Not once," Petey said confidently. There was a smug look on his face. He was overly prideful as if he had gotten away with something more impressive than skipping class. To Holden, this was no accomplishment. "The old bag in the office don't do her job right. The teachers send the attendance sheet down, but she don't look at it! We ain't never got a call home for playin' hooky."

Amused, Holden let out a chuckle. The thought excited him but given that it was his first day of school, Holden sighed. "I shouldn't miss my first day," he said in genuine disappointment.

Drew leaned over Petey and playfully punched Holden on the shoulder. "Come on," he said. "It ain't that big of a deal." Harry joined in on the peer pressure, looking at Holden with puppy dog eyes. Petey rubbed his fists on his cheeks to wipe away invisible tears.

With little contemplation, Holden said "Yeah, screw school." The other boys nodded their heads in approval of Holden's decision.

At that moment, the vehicle came to a halt outside a pitiful elementary school. The building was minuscule and looked nearly abandoned. Peeking from the window, Holden could see some of the school's playground. A single rusty basketball net arose from the pavement, which was uneven and cracked. There appeared to be some chalk drawings on that pavement, though the colour had been dulled. Moving his head further to the edge of the window, Holden could just see the bottom of a dented metal slide.

Children came into Holden's line of sight; they were starting to leave the vehicle. One by one, each child squeezed through the aisle before exiting the school bus. Holden and the others came out last. Once outside, Holden looked around some more in disbelief of his surroundings. Though, before he had a chance to bask in the grandeur of his brand-new school, Holden was pulled into one of the shrubs that lined the front of the school.

"Shh," said Petey as he covered Holden's mouth. Fearing that Petey's hands could be filthy, Holden pursed his lips while Drew and Harry squatted in the shrubbery alongside them. The four waited until a teacher – an older woman with starch white hair – appeared from inside the school. She beckoned for the children to come in, and so they did. After the last child had passed through the doors, the teacher did not bother to scan the area for any more students. She simply turned her back and shuffled into the building, the doors closing behind her with a thud.

Only a few seconds later, Petey stood up and began walking away. Immediately, Drew and Harry followed, leaving a confused Holden in their trail. The boys travelled quickly across the school's driveway and Holden struggled to catch up with them, which he eventually did. Not before long, small beads of sweat appeared on Holden's forehead. He was not used to such vigorous exercise. Despite the workout, just as hastily as he had met the boys' pace, he fell behind.

Holden was a few feet behind the others, so he bellowed out to them. "How long is it until we get there?"

"Jus' a minute," one of them called out. Holden was not quite certain which boy it was. They all sounded the same to him.

As he walked, Holden examined his new surroundings. He had never seen a forest so dreary and unmanicured. Right about now, the autumn leaves were beginning to ripen in color around Toronto, but the trees here were already bare. Despite there being no foliage to populate the towering trees, the forest was dark and lacked any sunlight. The forest was already unsettling, though the feeling was amplified by the eerie silence that loomed around them.

Caught up in his criticisms, Holden tripped on a branch and hit the ground hard. He began to rise and felt that he was out of breath. Holden remained kneeling on the dirt trail for a moment before finally standing, but it was too late – the other boys had moved on. Appalled at their lack of class, Holden considered abandoning the trek altogether. However, he soon realized that Petey and the others lead him into a foreign environment, and so only they would know the way out. Left with no other choice, Holden continued travelling forward in hopes of reconnecting with Petey, Harry and Drew. With each step, Holden drew closer into the forests' abyss, a crow flying high above him. He looked up and shivered.

"What the hell?" Holden yelled. After another few minutes of walking, he had finally reached the boys. They were in a clearing, sitting on large rocks and skipping stones into the water across from them. The boys started to laugh.

"Oh, you relax pal," Petey responded. "All that matters is that ya got here, right?" He gestured to Drew and Harry, who each nodded their head. Petey approached Holden and patted him on the shoulder;

an act that was a little too rough for Holden's liking. "It's a beauty, ain't it?"

In an attempt to vanquish his frustration and anger, Holden simply nodded and produced an artificial smile. Petey smiled back, though his smile was presumably authentic. Holden spied a large gap between his two front teeth and wondered why Petey never got braces. After all, braces are only a couple of thousand dollars. Holden's father had gotten them for him with no issues at all.

Petey backed away from Holden and jogged over to a hollowed log a few feet away. He bent down and reached inside to retrieve a slingshot before returning to the others. Holden stared at the device in Petey's hands – he had never seen a slingshot before.

"Are y'all ready to get your shootin' on?" Petey exclaimed.

The other boys hooted and hollered, both Drew and Harry leaving to fetch their targets. Petey sat confidently on a rock and waited for his goons to prepare their informal shooting range. Holden watched as Harry rolled over another large log into the clearing, while Drew carefully balanced soda cans onto its surface. When they were finished, they called Holden and Petey over.

“You ever use one of these before?” Harry asked Holden. As he spoke, he flashed the sleek wooden slingshot.

“I can’t say that I have,” he responded. Holden began to feel weary of his inexperience.

“Well, watch us a few times and then you can try. None of us are great shots, but it sure is a lot fun.”

Holden nodded his head and waited for one of the boys to start. Petey was now in possession of the slingshot and so he stepped forward. Petey knelt to the ground and searched for a small rock before readying himself for the first shot. He held the slingshot close to his face to better control his aim, though it was of no use. Almost immediately after the rock had been expelled from the slingshot, Holden could tell that it would miss the targets. The rock landed foul and a few feet short of the cans.

Drew and Harry were no different, each one carefully lining up their shot and failing miserably still. Once all the other boys had gone, Holden was handed the slingshot. He kneeled and picked up a few stones, selecting one whilst dumping the rest onto the ground. With his hands shaking, Holden aimed the slingshot at the first can to the left and fired. He hit the can dead on, knocking it over.

Holden was exhilarated, as were the others. Petey beckoned him to shoot again and so once more, Holden retrieved a rock and shot. This second shot seemed to have been launched with more force and accuracy than the one prior. Quickly, a grin appeared on Holden's face; he was releasing his anger, and doing it well, at that. Holden lunged to the ground for another rock, shooting this one of his own intense volition. The next can he aimed at was sent flying with a velocity that Petey and the others had never seen before. Holden continued to fire until there were no more tin cans on the shooting range.

"Do you have more?" Holden called out. His voice exerted an urgency that even Holden did not recognize.

"Uh, I guess we can reuse the ones you already hit," said Petey hesitantly.

Drew and Harry shuffled into the brush to retrieve the targets but returned with only three, which were heavily dented and disfigured. They balanced them back on the log and were barely out of range before Holden aimed to shoot again. The boys observed Holden as he focused on his aim, a delirious look of earnestness in his eyes. His gaze remained fixated on the shot as the rock catapulted through the air, knocking the can far backwards with a loud ding. It was at this moment that a flock of birds retreated from the forest with fear.

Their wings flapped in the near distance, propelling them higher and higher. Holden picked up some rocks and fired two shots at the birds, each of them successfully hitting their target. As the rest of their flock flew away, the two unfortunate victims cawed in pain and fell from the sky.

Watching in awe, every nerve in Holden's body felt stimulated. Then, all at once, Holden's demeanour calmed, and he let out a sigh that lasted a bit too long. From a few feet away, Petey and the others saw his muscles relax and it frightened them.

"Man, why in the world would you do that?" Drew exclaimed with a boom in his volume.

"That's just messed up," Petey added in, saying "we shouldn't have even taken you here."

"Yeah, what a city freak," concluded Harry.

Holden paid no attention to the remarks being made and instead started over to the vicinity of where the birds had fallen. Petey, Drew, and Harry took this as an opportunity to flee the scene, and so they ran rapidly into the forest without a second thought. Meanwhile, Holden continued his path until he found them – the two birds he had shot.

They were a few feet apart from each other, the one closest to him already dead. Holden assessed the damage he had done to the deceased bird, and saw that the rock had made an impact with its head. The bird was bloody, and its neck contorted from an evident break, but the sight did not process in Holden's mind as something to grieve. With his face mundane and devoid of any remorse, he stepped over its body to view the second bird.

Unlike the first, this bird was still alive after Holden had shot it. Despite its injuries, there was still life in this tiny creature. Holden watched as the bird struggled to lift itself off the ground; it could not do so, as Holden had broken its right-wing. Aside from the oddly positioned wing and its frayed feathers, the bird was quite beautiful. Its smooth coat of feathers was coloured black, but upon further inspection, there were also tints of a deep purple spread throughout its body.

After kneeling and looking into its eyes, Holden briefly considered leaving it be. The bird longingly looked back at him with its eyes opened wide. The sight almost made him want to desert the situation altogether – almost. Making eye contact with the bird, Holden realized that it was *because* of the creature's beauty that it needed to die. Holden's own eyes began to fill with rage. Why should the bird be saved? Because it is beautiful? Why does it get to be beautiful and free with no consequences?

Holden arose and scanned the area around him. After finding a substantially sized rock, he lifted it with all the strength he had in him and carried it until he was standing over the bird. Looking down at the injured animal, Holden did not waver. In one swift motion, he slammed the rock onto its helpless body. Promptly after he launched the boulder, he began to roll it over. The sight that emerged from underneath it was foul, with the bird's body flattened out onto blood-stained dirt. Without a doubt, the creature was dead.

Holden took a prideful look at the scene but was bothered by the deceased bird, who seemed to still be looking at him. Its now cold and lifeless eyes managed to retain their beauty, remaining stunningly dark. Staring back into those eyes, Holden could not help but think that they reminded him of something – or someone. Without giving it much thought, Holden turned and began walking back to where he thought he came from, a bird flying high above.

‘Til Death Do Us Part

DAY 30

It had almost been a month and the honeymoon phase still hadn’t died off. Although Dan and Casey Nolan had only just tied the knot, Casey knew that she had made the best decision of her life.

She and Dan had not known each other for very long before he proposed. But despite this, she could feel it in her heart that they were endgame; that, unlike her bitter, divorced parents, she and Dan would last.

The couple had not lived together until they wed, and Casey was still adapting to her new husband’s way of life. Dan snored – a lot. He was also messy and often forgot to put down the lid on the toilet seat. Despite Dan’s charm, he was a nightmare to live with. Casey supposed that she would have to tough it out and get used to it. After all, this was still the man of her dreams. Just like herself, Dan had flaws. In the near month that they had been husband and wife, Casey made it a habit to remind herself of this notion.

When Dan bought take-out on his way home from work, Casey had to do just that. He had not gotten her anything, and it was from their favourite Chinese place. “Sorry babe,” he mumbled. He had noodles in his mouth – *nom nom* – and he chewed as he spoke. “I must have forgotten.” *Nom nom nom*. “Maybe you can make some dinner here.”

“It’s alright,” Casey said sweetly. But it was not alright.

She had been sick with a cold and had not had the strength to go grocery shopping in over a week. Dan should have known very well that there was no food for her to make at home. Casey accepted that Dan worked long hours and had a lot on his plate, but it puzzled her as to how he would just forget about his wife. She had not liked the feeling of being forgotten, of being lost in the mix. That was the way things were when she was growing up and surely, she had gotten away from that.

"Here, I'll go check the fridge for you." Dan waltzed into the kitchen and flung open the fridge. From the couch, Casey studied his expression. When he saw the contents of the fridge, Dan's expression of enthusiasm faded.

Dan turned to face Casey and said, "Why haven't you gone shopping?"

"I've been sick, you know that" said Casey. He stared at her in disbelief, as if she were fabricating the whole thing. She thought that he would shoot out some sarcastic jabs, but he kept quiet. Dan said nothing for a moment.

"Well, it's getting late. I'm going to go to bed," Dan finally said. It was only 9:32 pm.

Casey did not know what to think. She had never seen Dan act like this before; they had never been in a such an awkward situation. In the moment, Casey felt like she did not even know Dan. But maybe she was wrong – maybe it was her that was the problem. She questioned if she had done something wrong, if she had been unintentionally milking her own sickness. So, Casey decided that the next day, she would go into town to buy some groceries, regardless of how she was feeling.

The next morning, she did just that.

After driving the fifteen minutes it took to get to the grocery store, Casey was already exhausted. She put her gas-guzzling car into park and hopped out, grabbing some reusable shopping bags from the back seat. Due to her poor parking spot, Casey travelled for a minute or two across the parking lot, before getting to the store.

4-Less-Foods was an independent grocery store, and a bad one at that. It was cramped, dingey, and had an extremely limited selection of groceries. Casey had never been there before but chose to go because it took less time than driving out to the bigger one. But as bad as 4-Less-Foods was, at least they were cheap.

Casey was a turtle as she moved through the maze of narrow aisles. Many sniffles later, she eventually got the necessities that she and Dan ate the most. Casey didn't have the strength to get any more than that, and so she went to purchase her groceries.

The lady at the check-out reeked of cigarette smoke. She had tried to cover it up with a cheap, drug-store perfume, but failed to do so. Her nametag said 'Kimberly' and she looked like an escort. Perhaps that was her side gig. Kimberly scanned Casey's groceries with haste and a dirty look, as if she were banishing Casey from the store.

Casey carried out her semi-filled grocery bags and walked to her car. She had only just begun to put her bags into the trunk when she felt something yank at her shoulder.

"Wha–"

"Shhh." When Casey turned around, there was a lady standing in front of her. She had dark brown hair, styled in a stylish bob. She looked to be in her thirties, though her winged eyeliner made her look significantly younger than that. The woman carried a designer bag, which made Casey feel poorly about herself. The only bags that she herself had were the ones under her eyes. Casey, in her sweats and messy bun, thought that she looked like crap compared to the beautiful stranger.

"Please," the woman said, "keep your voice down." Casey nodded and said nothing. "My name is Heather Nolan. I'm your husband's sister."

Casey's face contorted in confusion. She and Dan had always told each other everything, or so she thought. Dan told her that he was estranged from his parents and that other than them, he had no family members. If Heather was being truthful, then that had all changed. Dan would have had a sister.

Heather pulled out a wallet from that fancy purse of hers, flipping it open to reveal a driver's license – Heather Nolan. Looking at the picture on Heather's license, Casey really could see the resemblance to Dan. They both had the same dark hair and they shared eyes that were an identical shade of green. Like Dan, her body was lanky and thin. As was the case with Dan, Casey felt that in his sister's presence, she would blow her over if she were to exhale too much.

"Look," Heather said. "I have to tell you something and I have to make it quick. He could be watching."

"Who?" Casey asked with a chuckle.

Heather stepped closer to her and leaned in. Her already hushed voice turned to a whisper as she said, "Joseph."

Based off of the wild look in Heather's eyes, Casey decided that the woman in front of her was crazy. "Look, I don't know what you're talking about. I don't know a Joseph. Now, if you'll excuse me," she said. Casey finished packing the grocery bags and shut the trunk door.

"No, please. You have to hear me out."

"I don't know what you want, but-"

"I don't want anything but for you to be safe." There was a long pause. "I'm serious. Joseph is dangerous. But you know him as Dan, don't you?"

"Dan is my husband," Casey stated matter-of-factly.

"Exactly. And you aren't his first wife."

Casey gasped. She did not know if it was audible or not, but she knew that it happened. "What do you mean? He said he barely even dated before meeting me." Casey spoke in a flurry, fumbling over her words.

"Before you, there was Ava. And before Ava, there was Madison. He killed them both. Gunshot wound to the head – execution style. It was the way that our mom was killed all those years ago. It was our father who did it." Heather looked solemn, and so she took a moment to collect herself before continuing. "32 days. He waited 32 days before he murdered Madison, and the same went for Ava. I guess it was because our mom was 32 years old when she was killed. The cops eventually put that together.

"I'm just so glad that I found you in time. With Madison, no one expected it and it came as a tragic shock to everyone in our lives. But with Ava, I had a suspicion and I didn't act on it. I've regretted it ever since. When they found Ava's body, Joseph was already gone. He's the only suspect for both murders, but he fled. No one has been able to find him, until a week ago. My private investigator got me a lead that took me here to you. So, here I am."

Heather took out her cell phone and turned it to show Casey an album in her camera roll. Casey took the phone in her hand and started swiping. The pictures were screenshots of various online articles about the murders. Some of them had inserts of crime scene photos that had leaked into the public. Essentially, each photo was composed of the same components: caution tape, a dead wife, and blood. Lots of blood.

Casey's mind was spinning. She thought of sweet and caring Dan Nolan; her best friend and the man that she loved. That man could not have done all of this – but he did. The truth was right in front of her.

Then she pictured those poor women. She imagined the utter fear that must have gone through their heads, right before a bullet did. The thought made her feel even more ill than she had been from her cold. It was Dan who had done it; it was Dan who was going to do it again, to her. Casey turned pale as a ghost and her bottom lip was quivering. With shaky hands, she gave Heather back her phone.

"I know it's a lot to take in, but you have to try to stay calm. Like I said before, he could be watching. He's crazy. You don't want him to see you cry like this. He could break the pattern and act sooner."

"Okay," Casey said. She wiped a single tear, which had rolled slowly down her face. After it was gone, the tear-stained stream on her cheek glistened in the sunlight. She pulled it together and took out her own cell phone. Casey was about ready to call the police, but Heather stopped her.

"No!" Heather exclaimed. She realized how loud she had just been and quieted her voice once more. "No," she said again. "You can't do that. He can track your phone. You have to be smart with this, Casey. Hold off as long as you can until you make your move to leave. If necessary, wait until the night before your time is up."

Before your time is up.

Heather continued to speak, but Casey had already tuned out. Her eyes were glossy, and she could not focus on anything. Without saying another word, Casey moved past Heather and got into her car. Heather stood by in confusion as Casey flew past her. Within seconds, the car was being put into reverse and Heather abruptly stepped to the side. Casey drove out of the store parking lot and did not look back.

DAY 31

A day had passed, and Casey did not leave the downstairs couch. Her sniffles and sore throat were easing up, but her mind was not. She had slept on the couch the night prior, saying that she did not want to get Dan sick. He did not question it. In reality, she no longer felt safe sleeping in his arms. The couch was cramped and uncomfortable, but it was still better than being in the same bed as a killer.

She was glad that Dan worked today and that she did not have to see him until dinner time. But Casey hoped to be out of the house by then. That morning, after Dan had left for work, Casey had gone through the house and packed her most treasured belongings in a duffle bag. She did not want to take much more than that; multiple bags would slow her down.

In her only bag, Casey packaged one change of clothes, her phone charger, and some small personal belongings. While in their bedroom, she had left her wedding ring and engagement ring on the bureau. She could not stand to have the damned things on her any longer.

Every hour that passed, did so slowly. Casey had immense temptations to leave before her planned time, but ultimately, she did not. Like Heather said, Dan could be watching. For all Casey knew, he may not have even been at work. Instead, she stayed on that small, leather couch and watched trashy reality shows on the television. She tried to zone out; to imagine herself in some sort of a dream where none of this was happening. But not even badly tanned celebrities with botched plastic surgeries could make this nightmare go away.

DAY 32

It was midnight and Dan had not come home. Casey was thankful at first, but she then realized that he could be waiting for her; waiting to kill her. She spent hours beforehand contemplating whether or not it was the right time to make her move. Eventually, she procrastinated so much that it was 12:00 am and she was still at home. Dan was not.

When the clock on her phone hit 12:01am, Casey decided that it was time to go. She moved in a frenzy, trying to get her shoes and jacket on. She decided to sneak out of a bottom floor window, fearing that Dan would be at the front door, waiting. Casey walked quietly to the dining room and lifted the window with great caution. She stepped foot onto the grass, which was dewy from the rain earlier in the day. She almost slipped but recovered, reflexively holding onto the edge. She sighed in relief and closed the window.

Casey took a step forward and was struck on the head. Her body fell to the ground as completely dead weight. Heather grinned as she dragged Casey's body around the house and into the front hall.

When Casey awoke, she found herself to be back in her own living room. She was seated on the floor, propped up against the wall. Across the room were Dan and Heather, chatting eagerly but quietly. She got up and began to run to the front door, which was only a few feet away. A shot rang out. Casey fell to the ground; blood was already pooling around her. When she looked up, she saw that Heather was looming over her with a handgun.

Pain surged through Casey's body as she came to the realization that she had been shot. Her leg burned and she felt nauseous. Looking down at her leg, she saw that her jeans were a dark red, and the entirety of her right thigh was soaked with blood. Casey felt like she could not move, and so she remained still. There was no point in moving, anyways. She waited for one of them to say something, but the words never came – they both stayed silent. A look of smug satisfaction was on Dan's face. The face that Casey had once adored so much, now terrified her.

"Would you like to do the honors, Joseph?" she heard Heather ask.

"Why, of course."

Heather passed the gun to Dan, and he put it in his pocket. He then walked over to Casey as Heather watched from afar. Once he was closer, Dan eyed her down, a predator evaluating his prey. He yanked Casey up by her hair, commanding "Get on your knees."

He had pulled her hair so hard that a few strands came out in a knotted clump. Dan took the hair in his hand and blew it in Casey's face. It fell in front of her, with some strands getting caught in her bloody legs. Casey's wounded leg had turned numb, allowing her to kneel on the hardwood floor with little feeling. Once she was fully on her knees, Dan crouched down to be at eye-level with his wife. He looked Casey dead in the eyes and smiled a wicked smile, ear to ear. He gave her a wink and stood up. Dan ran his hand through his hair a few times before taking the gun out from his pocket. He held it casually, swinging it around for a few seconds.

Casey looked up at her husband, who was now a stranger. She wondered how she would look when her body was found; if there would be pieces of her brain blown out and scattered on the floor, or if her blood would be splattered onto the walls like an abstract painting. The sound of a gun cocking took her away from her swirling thoughts. Then the trigger was pulled, a bullet going right through her head, -and then Casey had no thoughts at all.

Brownie Bear

March 2nd, 2018

Eric and I moved into the new house yesterday, but Mom doesn't understand. When I visited her this morning, she kept going on about the previous homeowners.

"Whatever happened to that nice couple down the street?" she kept asking.

"They moved out, Mom. And I moved in to be closer to you." I must have said that upwards of ten times.

"Why would they ever do such a foolish thing? That's nonsense."

"Do you want to do our exercises?" I smiled when she accepted the offer.

Whenever I go over, she likes showing me family photos and playing the piano. She also enjoys doing crosswords, but not for long. Mom forgets how to hold the pencil properly half of the time. We did all of those things today, as well as an exercise that she isn't fond of. Once again, I asked her to tell me what she knows. She says it is insulting to her intelligence, and I say that intelligence has nothing to do with Alzheimer's Disease.

What Mom usually says is, "I know my name; I am Judy May Warren. I know your name; you are Vera Jean Warren. I know you are my daughter and I know you love me. I know I am your mother and I love you."

Today, she said, "I don't know what I know, but I know what I don't know."

What *I know,* is that she is plummeting. It's all downhill from here.

March 11th, 2018

Today marks two years since Mom was diagnosed. She managed it well enough until she couldn't, and I'm proud of her for that. When we first found out, Eric and I lived an hour away. I had asked Mom how she felt about going to a long-term-care home. She sobbed and swore for days. When we proposed that a nurse take care of her at home, she threatened to fire any support staff that set foot on her property. We had no other options, so Eric and I pulled the trigger. We bought the house across the street from her. Why? She is too Goddamn stubborn to have anyone else look after her. I love that stubbornness, though. It's one of the only traits that have stuck after all this time.

March 29th, 2018

Mom called my cell at 6:00 am today.

"I'm trying to remember the name of our dog," she yelled into the phone.

"What?"

"You know, the one from when you were in high school. I think it was a poodle, but maybe it wasn't. Anyways, what was its name? Billy? Bobby? Bella? Bueler?"

"It was Frankie, Mom. His name was Frankie."

"Ah, yes! That was it. I miss Frankie. I miss having someone stay in the house with me. It gets so lonely nowadays. Well, it's getting rather late. Goodnight, darling. I love you."

"Goodnight, Mom."

<u>April 14th, 2018</u>

We were going to have Mom over tonight. Eric made a nice chicken dinner with some roast beef on the side; Mom has always preferred beef over chicken.

I walked across the street to fetch Mom and bring her over. When she answered the door, she did a little dance and asked how she looked. Mom had put her hair in curlers but forgot to take half of them out. Her face was powdered, and she had painted her lips with a blotchy, red matte. Despite it being springtime, she had on her favorite coat and an ugly scarf I made her in the fifth grade. After all these years, Mom still wore it with pride.

How did she look? She looked more like Ronald McDonald than a Hollywood starlet, but that smile on her face made up for it. So, I told her, "Like a million bucks, Mom."

She held my hand going down the steps of her porch and linked arms with me once we began crossing the street, just as she had once done with me as a child. Mom pointed to the flowers starting to bloom and told me how pretty they were. She pointed to cars as they drove by and rebuked them for their irresponsible speed. As we approached home, Mom pointed to our house and stopped walking. She tilted her head slightly and let go of my hand, pointing both fingers at the house.

"What are we doing here?"

"This is my house. Eric made you a nice dinner, Mom. We're going to have your favorite, roast beef."

"No, this isn't right. That nice couple lives here but I can't remember who they are. I know who they are, but I can't remember them."

"Mom, please. Let's just go inside and have a nice hot meal. Eric is excited to see you."

"There isn't an Eric that lives here. It is polite young man with dark hair and his name is not Eric, I know that. I don't know who he is, but I know that isn't him." Her frustration was audible. "I'm not going anywhere until I know what happened to that nice young couple."

"They're gone, Mom."

"No! No! No! No! No! No! No! No!" she wailed.

The switch was like Dr. Jekyll and Mr. Hyde. She had never gotten angry like that before, and I didn't know what to do. I took a few steps towards her, but she stumbled backwards trying to avoid me. She told me to take her home, so I did. I stayed with her for an hour until she fell asleep, and then I departed.

By the time I got home, the chicken and roast beef were cold, and Eric had fallen asleep on the couch.

<u>April 21st, 2018</u>

Mom has been difficult with me. I went over today, and she refused to do any of our regular activities. She flipped the photo album out of my hands when I brought it to her and retreated into the bedroom.

There are no more 'good days', just varying degrees of bad days.

May 3rd, 2018

Today, Mom was scouring the phone book. I asked her what she was looking for, but she ignored me. I went on to point out that phone books are obsolete now.

"You're obsolete!" she barked, continuing to tear through the pages. "You won't tell me what happened to that nice couple down the street, so I'm going to find them myself."

I entertained the notion and offered to help her look, even though neither of us knew their names. In response, she threw it at me with such force that my arm bruised a bit.

"Just because I need you for everything doesn't mean I can't do something on my own."

I handed her the phone book again. I conceded and let her continue. She searched for six hours.

May 15th, 2018

This morning, I tried to get Mom to come over again, but she refused. When I went over in the evening, all the lights in her house were turned on. She wasn't in the living room or kitchen when I came in, so I called her name. In response, there was muffled crying.

I found her on the floor of her bedroom, holding a teddy bear and weeping.

"I remembered your Brownie bear tonight, for no good reason at all. He just popped into my mind, and I spent hours trying to remember which box he was in," she blubbered.

I joined her on the floor. "I haven't seen Brownie bear in a long while, I didn't even really remember him."

"You carried that bear with you everywhere for years and years, and I couldn't remember my daughter's favorite toy. He was such a big part of your childhood, and I didn't even remember he existed. I... I don't want to forget him again."

"I'm sure you'll remember him from now on," I lied.

"Vera, take him home with you. I want you to have him, please." She passed me Brownie bear; his caramel fur now spotted with tear stains.

"Sure, I'll take him. But I have to ask, why do you have all the lights turned on?"

I meant to brighten the mood, but it wasn't amusing for Mom. "If all the lights are on, then I won't be able to fall asleep, and if I don't fall asleep then I won't wake up tomorrow and I won't forget Brownie."

<u>May 30th, 2018</u>

Lately, Mom has been asking me to tell her stories from the past. Last night, I told her about our dog Frankie that was so dear to us both. I told her about my high school graduation and how she was so proud that she cried. I told her that when I first moved out, she sent care packages to my college dorm every week. I told her that she continued sending care packages, even after I married and moved into my own house. I told her that she is the best mother I could ever ask for and that I love her.

Mom looked at her feet and said, "I wish I was still the best mother."

June 22nd, 2018

Eric and I were at lunch when I got a call from Mom, only it wasn't Mom who had called me. It was an EMT. He didn't tell me exactly what was wrong, only that something *was* wrong.

We rushed to the hospital, and I wept the whole way. Once we arrived, they took us into her room where a doctor was waiting. He told us that Mom had wandered onto her front lawn, and that she was crying and hollering nonsense. One of the neighbors heard the commotion and came outside. Mom got scared and didn't know where she was or who she was, and she fainted. The neighbor thought she had a heart attack and called 911, but it turned out to be a severe panic attack.

Something like this happened last year, right before Mom's neighbors – the previous homeowners of my house – moved out. Judy and Patrick were newlyweds who grew increasingly uncomfortable with Mom's behaviour. She wasn't even that far gone yet, but they didn't like how she would stare at their house all day or how she sat on their lawn. I guess it got to be too much because they moved a few months after that.

Eric and I met with them when we bought the house. Judy didn't speak the whole time, and her husband spoke only once. "Good luck with her."

At the hospital, I signed some forms and gave him the information he needed to know. The doctor said that Mom needed her rest and wouldn't be awake for a bit, and that visiting hours ended soon anyways. Eric took me home for the night, but it didn't feel like home anymore. Not without Mom.

June 23rd, 2018

When I went to the hospital today, I brought Brownie bear with me. I waited in the hall until a nurse came out of Mom's room and told me I could go in.

Before I entered, she nodded towards me and whispered, "Miss. Judy has been chirping and chirping about some neighbors down the street. She gets kind of angry when you change the subject." I took note and continued in. Mom was sitting straight up in her bed, gazing out the window.

"Hey, mom," I said.

"Oh! Maybe you'll know something. Do you know what happened to that nice couple on my street? I haven't seen them in ages."

"I don't know, I'm sorry."

"No one is any help around here. You nurses are all the same."

I walked towards her bed and offered her Brownie bear. She looked at him with glossy eyes and brought him into her grasp. Mom's face turned red as she examined it; that's when she started tearing him a part.

"I don't want your stuffed rabbit. It doesn't even look like a bloody rabbit." Mom threw Brownie bear's head on the ground, and I began to cry. "Who in the heck are you anyway? Get out, get out of my room!"

My heart sank.

Mom started yelling for help, yelling that there was a stranger. The nurses swarmed her room and escorted me out. I didn't try to stop them. When I turned around, they were already closing the door. Through the narrowing crack, I saw a nurse sweeping up Brownie bear's stuffing and dumping it into the garbage bin.

It's finally happened: Mom is completely senile. Still stubborn, but senile, nonetheless. She doesn't know who she is, and she doesn't know who I am. She tore Brownie bear until his stuffing spilled onto the tile and his body was nothing but a shapeless, lifeless form.

Just like Brownie bear, ~~Mom's~~ Judy May Warren's memories have spilled out of her mind and into oblivion. She is hollow, like an unstuffed teddy bear: an empty husk of what once was.

About the Author

Jordan Murray is a writer from Toronto, Canada. *Bird Boy: and Other Short Stories* is her first published work.

As of 2021, Murray is currently a university student majoring in English Literature. When she is not writing, she can be found reading or playing the piano.

She is currently working on a full-length novel of her own in the genre of adult psychological thriller/suspense.

www.ingramcontent.com/pod-product-compliance
Lightning Source LLC
Chambersburg PA
CBHW020524310726
48979CB00014B/2203/J

* 9 7 8 1 7 7 7 1 0 6 0 2 7 *